STECK-VAUGHN

PAIR-IT BOOKS™

W9-CNL-637

Dinosaur Fun Facts

Written by Ellen Keller

STECK-VAUGHN
COMPANY

A Division of Harcourt Brace & Company

Some dinosaurs were tall.

Brachiosaurus was as tall as a tower.

Some dinosaurs were small.

Heterodontosaurus was as small as a dog.

Some dinosaurs were long.

Stegosaurus was longer than a camper.

Some dinosaurs were heavy.

Triceratops was as heavy as 2 elephants.

Some dinosaurs ate only plants.

Plant eaters had very flat teeth.

Some dinosaurs ate only meat.

Meat eaters had very sharp teeth.

Many dinosaurs were like lizards.

Dinosaurs do not walk on Earth today.

But you can see them in museums.